Losers beware!

"Okay, all the shirts are going to say THE STARS ARE THE GREATEST on the front," Amy said. "I think we should write it in orange or red so people can see it from far away."

"I'm going to outline mine in sequins," Sara decided. "The Clovers will absolutely hate it," she said cheerfully.

"I'm going to put green and purple polka dots on mine," Karen said. "Like the flag of planet Zigblat."

"Just remember, the *uglier* the better," Jan reminded them.

Other Books about the Fifth Grade Stars

Fifth Grade S·T·A·R·S
THE GOOFY GAMBLE

By Anna Jo Douglas

Bullseye Books · Alfred A. Knopf
New York

For Alyssa, Doug and Anna Jo—
my stars

DR. M. JERRY WEISS, Distinguished Service Professor of Communications at Jersey City State College, is the educational consultant for Bullseye Books. A former chair of the International Reading Association President's Advisory Committee on Intellectual Freedom, he travels frequently to give workshops on the use of trade books in schools.

Library of Congress Cataloging-in-Publication Data
Douglas, Anna Jo
The goofy gamble / by Anna Jo Douglas. Cover art by Susan
Tang. p. cm.—(Fifth grade Stars ; #6)
Summary: Losing a bet may mean losing their clubhouse to the
Clovers when the Fifth Grade Stars compete against a rival
clique on Field Day. ISBN 0-679-80062-X [1. Clubs—Fiction.
2. Schools—Fiction] I. Title. II. Series: Fifth grade
Stars ; #6. PZ7.C16167Go 1989 [Fic]—dc19 89-2634

RL: 5.4
Manufactured in the United States of America

1 2 3 4 5 6 7 8 9 10

Fifth Grade S·T·A·R·S

THE GOOFY GAMBLE

◀ 1 ▶
Tofu to You Too

When Amy Danner woke up on Tuesday morning, she just didn't want to go to school. It was a gorgeous spring day. The curtains on her bedroom window were open halfway, and there was no mistaking the clear blue sky and bright sunlight.

She groaned and rolled on her side. Her thick brown hair, messy from sleeping, tumbled over her eyes. Perfect weather—that meant at River Grove Elementary School it would be field day, as scheduled. An event that Amy dreaded.

Even though she was in the fifth grade, today would be the first time Amy had ever taken part in a school field day. She had moved to Sugar Tree Acres last summer and at her old school in the city, there hadn't been too much emphasis on sports.

Wednesday had been field day for the fourth grade, and tomorrow would be the sixth grade's turn. The entire school was so excited about field day that Amy thought it was absolutely weird. At her old school nobody had thought sports were such a big deal. But here in River Grove, it was different. Most kids thought being a good athlete was really cool.

The way her friends had explained it, field day was like a mini-Olympics, with all the classes in one grade competing in different events. But Amy still couldn't quite picture it. Her mother said that new experiences were always a little scary because you didn't know what to expect. Amy never liked to admit when she felt afraid. But she knew she'd rather spend a weekend at the dentist than go to school today. She would even wear pleated skirts and loafers for a month. And that was saying something.

Amy had her own unique ideas about fashion. The outfit she'd worn yesterday was still heaped on a chair—a neon-green jumpsuit that said FLIGHT SQUAD in orange letters on the back, a wide pink belt, and black high-top sneakers that she had splattered with Day-Glo yellow, orange, and pink paint. Her earrings, which Amy had made herself, were pieces of colored telephone wire with tiny plastic dinosaurs hanging off the ends. She had forgotten to take them off last night and she could feel the dinosaurs tangled in her hair.

No dinosaur earrings or jumpsuits today. Just boring old shorts or a jogging suit. That's what everyone would be wearing.

Amy sighed and pulled the pillow over her head. She could hear the TV on in the living room and her mother exercising with a morning show called *Wake-Up Workout with Wanda Monroe*.

"Kick a little higher now!" Amy recognized Wanda's perky voice. "Pick up the pace!"

Then she heard her mother, panting a bit as she kicked and counted along, "Two . . . and three . . . and four . . ."

Amy felt like there was a flock of butterflies in her stomach doing a wake-up workout with Wanda. Maybe she could tell her mother she felt sick and stay home. But her mother, who was a lawyer, wasn't so easy to fool. It would be tricky. . . .

"Amy? It's so quiet up there. Aren't you up yet?" her mother called from down the hall.

"I'll be right down!" Amy hollered back. Sometimes she could have sworn her mom could read her mind.

"Your breakfast is almost ready, honey. Pick up the pace."

Finally Amy dragged herself out of bed and went into the bathroom. Instead of pajamas she was wearing a huge T-shirt with her favorite rock star's picture on it—King Zero. She pulled it over her head and started to wash up.

Amy knew she wasn't *so* bad at sports. Not as bad as, say, her friend Karen Fisher, who was always the last one picked when they chose up sides in gym. But Amy was far from the athletic type. She was smart in school and really loved art, or any subject where she could use her imagination. When she grew up, she wanted to design clothes and jewelry, or make movies.

The problem was that everyone expected her to be good at sports because last sum-

mer she had
dian woods an
in the wilderne
mother had thou
women to learn to
learned a lot abou
in the woods off wil
she still didn't know
ball. It didn't matte
usually.

Except for today. If s   up, her
whole class would be wat   ng. Including
the boys. She only hoped she didn't get that
many chances to look foolish.

Amy dressed in black baggy shorts and
a pink-and-purple tie-dye T-shirt. Then she
put on her splattered black high tops and
turquoise socks. "Field day, here I come,"
she mumbled to herself. She'd try to do the
best she could and hope that by tomorrow
everyone would have forgotten who had won
what.

Down in the kitchen her mother was fix-
ing a cup of herbal tea. "Hurry and eat your
breakfast, honey. You don't want to miss
the bus."

Amy stared down at her plate.

"No offense, Mom . . . but what is it?"

was a genuine health-food
today for breakfast she'd fixed
ing pretty weird looking. It was big,
e, and very lumpy. It also had a few
scorched-looking tread marks, as if a truck
had just run it over, Amy thought.

"It's a tofu-and-blueberry waffle. You
know, I've made them for you before," her
mother said patiently. Amy recognized her
mother's not-another-food-discussion-please
voice. "It'll give you a lot of energy."

Amy sighed and started to eat. Tofu—
another name for soybean curd—was the
basic ingredient of practically every recipe
her mother cooked these days. It was sup-
posed to be good for you, but Amy was getting a little tired of it. Before her parents
got divorced, she and her dad would make
up tofu jokes—like one of them would shout,
"Toe-foo!" and the other would say, "Ge-
sundheit!" It was really corny, but it put a
secret smile on Amy's face every time she
had to eat the stuff.

Amy took a few nibbles of the gooey blue
waffle, then slipped a big hunk to her dog,
Oatmeal, who was staring at her beseech-
ingly from under the kitchen table. Oat-

meal gobbled up the waffle eagerly, then made a funny growling sound.

"Got to go," Amy said, grabbing her book bag and lunch.

"Good luck in field day today," her mom said. "I know you'll do real well."

"Thanks, Mom." Amy tried to sound more confident than she really felt. She knew her mother expected it.

At the bus stop Amy saw two of her best friends, Karen Fisher and Jan Bateman, waiting for her.

Together with Sara and Beth Greenfield, the five girls had formed a club called the Stars. They had all moved into the Sugar Tree Acres development last summer and had met on the first day of school at the bus stop. Amazingly enough, they were in Mr. Carson's class together too. It didn't take long before they became best friends.

As usual, Karen was reading a book. From the exploding planets on the cover Amy could tell that Karen was devouring another sci-fi story. Off in another galaxy, Karen didn't even notice Amy sneaking up right behind her. Jan covered her mouth with her hand to keep from laughing.

"Earth to Karen, Earth to Karen . . . Can you read me?" Amy said in a squeaky, outer-space voice.

"Huh? What was that?" Startled, Karen spun around and dropped her book. Then she saw it was only Amy. "Hey! I didn't even see you there."

"I didn't mean to scare you." Amy and Jan laughed, then Karen laughed too. Amy picked up Karen's book and gave it back to her.

"I wasn't scared. . . . Well, maybe for a second," Karen admitted. Taller than Amy and Jan, Karen had soft blond hair and spoke in a quiet voice. "Wow—I love your new T-shirt. Did you make it yourself?"

Amy nodded proudly. "I figure if I can't beat the competition, maybe I can distract them."

"That shirt should do it all right," Jan said.

Karen smiled. She was a little nervous about field day, and her friends' jokes made her feel better. Maybe Amy was nervous about today too. People always expected Karen to be good at sports because she was tall and rangy. But she'd much rather read a book any day than run up and down a basketball court, trying to get a dumb ball through a tiny hoop.

"I just hope I don't do something really klutzy and make our class lose," Karen said, twisting a piece of her long hair.

"You'll do fine," Amy promised. "Just remember, the other team is more afraid of you than you are of them."

"You're really not that bad when you try, Karen," Jan encouraged her. Jan liked sports and was especially good at volleyball. Her father was a coach at Crestview High School, and her brother was the star quarterback of the high school football team. It only made sense that she was the most athletic of her friends.

"Thanks, you guys—all I can do is try my best, I guess," Karen said with a shrug.

Karen thought her friends were the greatest. If she was on their team in gym, they never got mad at her if she dropped the ball or ducked when someone threw to her. They knew it wasn't her thing.

"I don't know about you, but I'm psyched," Jan said. She was wearing a pink hooded sweatshirt and gray sweatpants that had white stripes down each leg. Her straight brown hair was pulled back in a high ponytail, and she had a pink terry band around her head, under her bangs. "My brother helped me practice broad jumping last night. But it was hard to land on the living room carpet. I kept sliding into the piano."

"You practiced in the house?" Karen asked. Her parents were both scientists and liked the house to be as quiet as a library. She couldn't even imagine broad jumping across her living room.

"Only until my mom said it sounded like the house was falling down. Beth is running in the fifty-yard dash. She said she was getting up early to practice in her backyard—"

"The winner—Beth Greenfield!" As if on cue, Beth came streaking up to the bus stop. She raced past her friends with her arms over her head like she'd just won a gold medal in the Olympics. Holding her lunch bag in one hand and her loose-leaf notebook in the other, she looked pretty funny.

"Yay, Beth!" Karen shouted.

"Way to go!" Amy said.

"Thank you, thank you." Beth bowed, as if she heard an entire stadium applauding. "No autographs—please," she added in a serious tone.

"Yeah, before you know it my sister's

picture will be on a box of Wheaties." Beth's identical twin, Sara, hadn't been far behind and greeted her friends with a big smile.

The Greenfields both had wildly curly red hair and about a million freckles each. When they got embarrassed, angry—or had been running around like Beth was just now—their cheeks got bright red.

If you didn't know Beth and Sara, it was almost impossible to tell them apart. But their personalities were as different as night and day. Beth was outgoing and impulsive. She loved to joke around and act silly. She adored animals and had so many pets her father called their house the Greenfield Zoo.

Quiet and dreamy, Sara was the complete opposite. She liked to be alone a lot to think and write in her secret notebook. With five kids in the Greenfield family it was hard to find privacy, and Sara had a special tree in the backyard that she sat in when she needed some peace and quiet. Sara wanted to be either a writer or a private detective when she grew up. She was always making notes about people she met or jotting down ideas for the novel she was going to write someday.

Sara's novel was going to be about a

beautiful red-headed orphan called Tiffany
Vandermere who was madly in love with a
handsome pirate named Sean MacNeill.
Sean wasn't really a pirate, but he had to
pretend to be one for a while, which was
why he and Tiffany couldn't get married.
Sara hadn't quite figured out why Sean
was pretending to be a pirate. But she
knew writers had to work out these minor
details.

"What was my time, Sara?" Beth turned
to her sister.

"Twenty seconds," Sara replied, checking
her watch.

"That was from our front door," Beth explained between deep breaths. "But I had
to stop and tie my shoelace."

"Not bad," Jan said.

"I don't care if I win," Beth confessed, "as
long as I beat the shorts off Holly Hudnut."

At the mere mention of Holly all the Stars
made a face.

"I didn't know Holly was chosen to be in
the fifty-yard dash," Amy said.

"Well, she was," Jan said. "And I hope
you beat her, too, Beth." Jan's father had
taught her that good sportsmanship was
important. But Holly was another story.

Holly Hudnut acted like she was the greatest thing to come along since chocolate chocolate-chip ice cream. She was pretty, in a blond-haired, blue-eyed, kewpie doll sort of way and had nice clothes too. But the Stars still couldn't figure out why Holly Hudnut treated everybody like she was queen of River Grove Elementary School.

She acted so polite and helpful around grownups that a person who really knew her could absolutely gag. The whole fifth grade knew Holly was sneaky and mean. She loved to get other kids in trouble while she played the part of a perfect angel.

Holly had a club called the Clovers with her rich, snobby friends, and of course she was president. The Clovers were all in Mr. Carson's class too. At first the girls who were new to River Grove wondered if the Clovers would invite them to join their club. But it didn't take long for Holly to decide that the girls from Sugar Tree Acres didn't have a freckle of a chance to be a Clover. Holly thought that kids from Sugar Tree Acres were rejects, and naturally all of Holly's clone-head friends agreed.

It was Amy's idea to start a new club with

Jan, Karen, Beth, and Sara. They decided to call it the Stars because they all took the bus with the S.T.A.R. sign in the window, which stood for Sugar Tree Acres Route.

The great thing about the Stars was that they were *real* best friends. Not like Holly's phony gang, who always bossed each other around and talked behind each other's backs. The Stars always had a good time together. No matter how hard the Clovers tried to show the Stars up, they had never gotten the best of them yet.

"Watch out for Holly. She'll probably cheat and try to trip you while you're running or step on the back of your sneakers," Amy warned Beth.

"Just let her try," Beth said.

"All those Clovers are pretty sneaky if you ask me," Sara added. "Remember what they did to us at Lake Laverne?"

She was thinking of the time the Stars had gone camping and the Clovers had coincidentally showed up there too. One afternoon while the Stars were taking showers, Holly and her friends had sneaked into the dressing room and stolen all their bathing suits and towels.

"Sneaky or not, this is one day when the Clovers will have to behave because we're all on the same side," Karen pointed out. "It's just like this book I read about these two rival space colonies who are mortal enemies. But then they have to join forces to fight off the invaders from Zigblat who want to rule the entire universe."

"The only difference is Holly Hudnut already thinks she rules the entire universe," Amy said.

Everyone laughed. But it was something to think about. The Stars and the Clovers would all be playing for the same team during field day. It would be the first time the two rival groups ever had to cooperate and work together. Would it make them friendlier? Or would it start an all-out war?

◀ 2 ▶

Let the Games Begin!

The bus ride to school that morning was pretty rowdy. Pete McBride and Matthew Ellis, two boys in Mr. Carson's class, started up a chant.

"Carson's class is number one! Carson's class shall overcome! Number one! Overcome!"

All the other kids in Mr. Carson's class joined in, shouting and stomping their feet on the floor of the bus. Then a bunch of kids from Mrs. Gooley's fifth-grade class started chanting back, "Gooley's class is the best! Gooley's class will beat the rest!"

Finally the bus driver, Mrs. Purvis, pulled the bus over to the side of the road and told everyone they would spend field day in Mrs. Campesi's office if they didn't quiet down.

"Leave it to Pete McBride to get the entire bus sent to the principal's office," Amy whispered to Jan.

Pete McBride was one of the most popular boys in the fifth grade. He was short, but cute and smart. He liked to clown around and got in trouble a lot with Mr. Carson. Pete would always act shocked when Mr. Carson caught him. But for a guy who never did anything wrong, Pete was sent down to Mrs. Campesi's office all the time. Last week, Mr. Carson even suggested Pete move his desk down there.

Pete's best friend, Matthew Ellis, was quieter, but got in trouble sometimes because of Pete. Matthew was tall and gangly with ears that stuck out too far. He tried to comb his hair in a way that made his ears less noticeable, but it only looked worse. Matthew was one of the smartest kids in the fifth grade and a real whiz at Nintendo games. Being best friends with Pete made him popular too. He lived across the street from Amy, and he was always asking to borrow a pen or pencil from her in class. Jan thought Amy liked him a little, even though she swore she didn't.

In the classroom everyone was excited and eager to go outside. Mr. Carson was in the hall, talking to the other teachers, and nobody took a seat when the bell rang.

As usual, the Clovers were huddled up around Holly. They all wore their hair in the same style, a side ponytail. Today they had on the exact same outfit for field day too, bright yellow leggings with white stripes down the legs and bright yellow slouch socks that drooped stylishly over their running shoes. On top they all wore a matching oversized sweatshirt. There was a little white antelope sewn on the sleeve, so there was no mistaking the hot brand.

"Oh, gross! I can't believe it. I must be having a fashion nightmare." Amy covered her eyes with her hand. "Do you see what I see?" she asked the other Stars.

"A bunch of bananas with side ponytails?" Beth replied.

"Very funny, Beth Greenfield." Brenda Wallace turned around and made a face at Beth. Brenda was Holly's best friend. She had a long, horsy-looking face and hardly ever smiled. "Let's see if you're still laughing when Holly beats you in the fifty-yard dash."

"She'd better bring your horse," Sara snapped back. She usually didn't like to trade put-downs with the Clovers, but she had to defend her sister.

The other Clovers—Mary Rose Gallagher, Roxanne Sachs, and Sue Pinson—all looked at Holly, wondering what she'd say back.

"Oh, don't pay any attention to her," Holly told her friends in her fake, I'm-just-*so*-mature voice. "They're all total clods. I only hope they don't make our class lose today," she added just loud enough for everyone to hear.

"Especially Karen Fisher," Roxanne said. "Ever see her play volleyball? She acts like the ball will explode if she hits it. If it comes anywhere near her, she runs away."

All the Clovers started laughing, and Karen's cheeks got red. She looked down at her sneakers, and Jan thought she might cry. Jan didn't know what to say and just squeezed Karen's arm.

Karen had thought the Clovers might act nicer today, but she certainly didn't think so now.

Mr. Carson came into the room and clapped his hands, his signal to settle down. He was strict sometimes, but never raised his voice.

"Okay, line up folks and we'll go outside," he said. For once the class got in line faster than if it was a fire drill.

When they got outside, Mrs. Gooley's and Mrs. Krup's classes were already there, standing under the big trees near the baseball field. After Mr. Carson's group arrived, Mrs. Franks and Mr. Rocco, their gym teachers, took charge.

The girls and the boys split up, but the events they would compete in were the same. Some were team sports, like a relay race and a tug-of-war. Then there was the fifty-yard dash, high jumping, and broad jumping. Two girls and two boys had been chosen to represent each class in those events. The classes earned points for placing first, second, or third. The class with the most points won.

"The first event will be the fifty-yard dash. If I call your name, come up front," Mrs. Franks announced.

"Here goes nothing," Beth whispered to her friends.

"Good luck, Beth," Sara said.

"Yeah, Beth. Go for it," Jan told her.

"—Beth Greenfield, Holly Hudnut," Mrs. Franks said.

Beth heard her name, but she hesitated before going up to the starting line.

"Ummm—it feels kind of hot out. I'd better take off these sweatpants." She looked a shade paler under her freckles. Sara wondered if her twin—who had been raring to go this morning at the bus stop—was having a last-minute attack of stage fright.

Balancing on one leg, Beth started to pull off her sweatpants. Holly was already on her way up front. Passing by the Stars with her nose in the air, she accidentally-on-purpose bumped into Beth and sent her flying, her feet tangled in her sweatpants. "What's the matter, Beth?" Holly asked, looking down at her. "Tripping all over yourself so soon? The race didn't even start yet."

By the time Beth knew what had hit her, Holly was up front next to Mr. Rocco, picking out the best position on the starting line. Amy and Sara helped Beth up.

"That sneaky little worm!" Beth fumed. Her cheeks were beet red. "I'll show her!" she vowed as she marched off in an angry huff.

"Go get 'em, Beth!" Karen cheered.

"Go for it!" Jan and Amy called after her.

"I think Holly just pushed Beth too far," Karen said with a happy laugh. "Beth is so mad, she could run all the way to town and back in no time flat!"

"Yeah! Look at her," Amy said, pointing to Beth up at the starting line. She was taking her position with a very determined expression on her face. "I can practically see steam coming out of her ears!"

"Let's go up to the finish line and watch from there," Jan suggested. The other Stars thought that was a good idea and quickly ran to the far side of the field before the race began.

With a sharp blow of her whistle, Mrs. Franks signaled the start of the fifty-yard dash. The three classes of fifth graders roared, cheering on the runners they wanted to win.

The Stars were standing right near the finish line and cheered Beth on at the top of their lungs. Mr. Rocco was standing by with his stopwatch as the runners dashed down the field.

Just as Karen had predicted, Holly's plan to rattle Beth had backfired. Backfired on Holly and fired up Beth! With her red hair flying out behind her like a banner and her legs pumping for all she was worth, Beth streaked across the finish line first.

"First place—Beth Greenfield!" Mr. Rocco shouted for everyone to hear.

She swooped past her friends with her arms up in the air just as she had at the bus stop. Only this time she wasn't just pretending to be the winner.

Everyone in Mr. Carson's class—except for the Clovers—gave Beth a gigantic cheer.

"Way to go, Greenfield!" Pete McBride yelled. "Number one! Number one!" he shouted, repeating the rally cry he'd started on the bus.

The Stars were thrilled and gathered around her. "Wow, Beth! You did it! You really did it!" Amy and Jan jumped up and down.

"Yeah—I guess I did," Beth said, still panting. She seemed the most surprised of anyone as Mrs. Franks pinned a blue ribbon on her T-shirt. "And the funny part is, I have only Holly Hudnut to thank."

Mrs. Gooley's class came in second, and Mrs. Krup's class placed third. Holly came in fourth. Naturally, she had an excuse.

"No fair. I wasn't even ready," the Stars heard her whining to her friends. "I had a humongous pebble in my sneaker and I called time, but that stupid Mrs. Franks didn't listen to me."

The boys' race was about to start, and even the rest of the Clovers weren't paying much attention to Holly. Pete McBride and Tommy Tyler were running in the race from Mr. Carson's class. Probably because Pete was short, nobody really expected him to be tough competition. But as soon as the race started he shot ahead of the others and won by a mile.

"Pete McBride, first place," Mrs. Franks announced, and once again Mr. Carson's class had good reason to cheer.

Matthew Ellis and a bunch of Pete's other friends gave each other a high-five and then a low-five, like baseball players did when they scored a big home run.

"I knew Pete had a motor-mouth," Jan whispered to Amy. "But I didn't know he had legs to match."

"He reminded me of a runaway gerbil," Beth said. "Low to the ground, but *speedy*." She didn't mean anything insulting by it, though. She loved animals so much that comparisons to people automatically came to mind. In fact, if Beth compared a person to an animal, it was usually her way of giving a compliment.

The two boys from Mrs. Gooley's class came in second and third. When Mr. Rocco added up the points for each class, Mr. Carson's class was five points ahead of Mrs. Gooley's.

The broad jumping and high jumping were next, and the contests were run simultaneously. The Stars stayed at the broad-jumping pit to watch Jan and cheer for her. The Clovers were there too, cheering for Mary Rose Gallagher.

Each girl got three turns to jump. Jan's last jump was her best—she seemed to be flying through the air for the longest time before she landed at the far end of the sand pit.

Mary Rose was one of the most athletic girls in the fifth grade, and her height gave her a good advantage over the others. She beat Jan's best jump by only a few inches. Alice Nitsky from Mrs. Gooley's class was the very best, though. She came in first, with Mary Rose second and Jan a very close third.

The Clovers gathered around to congratulate Mary Rose. "Nice going," Holly said. "I knew you'd beat Jan Bateman," she added, talking more to the Stars than to Mary Rose.

"She only beat her by two measly inches," Amy pointed out. "Jan can't help it if Mary Rose is another Big Foot."

Mary Rose—who was otherwise *almost* as all-around perfect as Holly—did have big feet. She scowled at Amy, with her hands on her hips.

"Better than being from a nowhere neighborhood, like all of the Stars," Roxanne cut in. It wasn't much of a defense of Mary Rose's feet, but Roxanne knew the Stars hated it when the Clovers made fun of their neighborhood.

"Girls, please split up into class teams

for the relay race," Mrs. Franks said, making them move along before they could trade any more put-downs.

"I don't know how many points our class has, compared to the others. But it looks like so far it's Stars two, Clovers one," Amy pointed out.

"Don't pay any attention to them, Jan. You were really great," Karen said. "I couldn't have jumped half as far as you did. And neither could Holly."

"Thanks, Karen," Jan said. She really didn't care about Holly's wisecracks. She was happy to have gotten a ribbon and earned some points for her class. Her friends were excited for her, and that made Jan feel really good.

Jan's family had moved four times in the past four years. At every new school, Jan faced the same old story. She had to make new friends and try to fit in.

Because of her father and brother, other kids automatically assumed she was a jock. Jan liked gym and was pretty good at most sports she tried. But the funny thing was, her idea of a great time after school wasn't shooting baskets in the driveway with her big brother, Richie. It was cooking, the one thing she did better than anyone in her family or any of her friends.

Jan always thought of herself as average—average brown hair and brown eyes, average grades. But once she got into a kitchen she was a star, just like her TV chef idols, Julia Child and Chef Hubert, the Ragin' Cajun Cook. She loved to cook exotic dishes for her family and even imagined she might own a restaurant someday.

Coming in third in broad jumping wasn't so awful, Jan thought as she and her friends walked over to the relay race. She looked down at the yellow ribbon pinned to her T-shirt and knew she'd be proud to show it off when she got home.

The relay race was fun, and everybody got to participate. Each girl or boy had to dribble a soccer ball around three orange traffic cones, then turn around and dribble it straight back to the next person on their team.

The Stars stood in line together so that they got to pass the ball to each other. They didn't have to worry about the Clovers trying to mess them up and make them look clumsy. Mrs. Krup's class came in first, Mr. Carson's second, and Mrs. Gooley's third.

"Before we go on to the tug-of-war, here are the scores so far," Mrs. Franks said, looking down at her clipboard. "Mr. Carson's class has 30 points, Mrs. Gooley's has 25 points, and Mrs. Krup's has 20."

Mr. Carson's class jumped up and down, cheering for themselves, and then so did Mrs. Gooley's and Mrs. Krup's. The noise was so loud, Karen finally put her hands over her ears. It seemed as if all the kids thought the class that made the most noise would be declared the winner.

But there was still the tug-of-war. Mrs. Gooley's class and Mrs. Krup's faced each other first. Mr. Carson's class stood by watching and cheering for Mrs. Krup's class to beat Mrs. Gooley's.

No such luck. Mrs. Gooley's class gave a few good tugs and beat Mrs. Krup's class easily. They now had 35 points and Mr. Carson's class had only 30.

The moment of truth had arrived. The winner of the tug-of-war between Mr. Carson's and Mrs. Gooley's class would be the winning class of field day.

Pete McBride asked Mrs. Franks for a time-out so that Mr. Carson's class could have a huddle. Everyone squeezed around

Pete, who seemed to have declared himself team captain.

"The girls should be in the front, boys in the back. When I give the signal, go for it," Pete told the rest of the class.

It wasn't a very original plan, Amy thought. But at least it was something. The Clovers lined up together toward the front and the Stars lined up behind them. As Pete had suggested, the boys were in the back.

Mrs. Gooley's class didn't seem to have any plan, and when Mrs. Franks said to get ready, all the kids in that class just grabbed a piece of the rope.

Mr. Rocco blew the whistle, and the two classes started tugging with all their might. Amy gritted her teeth. Jan could feel her arms aching, and Sara dug her heels in the dirt to keep from sliding forward and giving ground. Karen was having the most trouble, but she squeezed her eyes closed and pulled with all her might.

For a second, it looked like Mr. Carson's class was going to win. The rope trembled and seemed to move a fraction of an inch in Mr. Carson's class's direction. Then Pete McBride yelled, "Harder! Now!"

The rope gave a gigantic lurch, which would have won field day for Mr. Carson's class—if Holly Hudnut hadn't stepped backward onto both of Karen's feet.

"Ouch!" Poor Karen gave out one painful screech before she was knocked onto the ground.

She fell backward into Amy, who fell into Beth, who landed on top of Sara, who couldn't avoid falling down on top of Jan. Holly—who had started the entire chain reaction—managed to nimbly jump clear of the pileup.

Each of the girls cried out in surprise. To the kids who were watching, they looked like a tumbled set of dominoes. While half of Mr. Carson's class was on the ground, Mrs. Gooley's class gave one sharp tug and won field day.

Mr. Rocco blew his whistle to signal the end of the tug-of-war and Mrs. Gooley's class went wild, cheering for themselves, "Gooley's class is the greatest! Gooley's class is the greatest!"

Karen and the other girls got up off the ground and brushed themselves off. All the kids in Mr. Carson's class felt bad about finishing second. But nobody felt worse than the Stars.

"You stupid clods! You made us lose!" Holly yelled, turning to the Stars.

"I wouldn't have fallen down if you hadn't stepped on my feet, Holly!" Karen said, defending herself. Her voice got even softer when she argued with someone.

"I did not!" Holly argued back.

"That's ridiculous. When did Karen Fisher ever need any *help* being clumsy?" Brenda asked the other Clovers.

It was time to go to the lunchroom, but the whole fifth grade was gathered around the Clovers and the Stars, waiting to see what would happen next.

"Okay, people. That's it. Time for lunch," Mrs. Franks said, trying to move the fifth graders along again.

Mr. Carson was standing with her. "I know we all feel bad about missing first place," he said to his class. "But this was a team effort. Win or lose, no single person is to blame. We came in second, and that's great," he added with a smile. "Now let's just cool off and have lunch."

Holly made a sour-looking face and

crossed her arms over her chest. It looked like she was dying to say something else mean about Karen but didn't want to get in trouble with Mr. Carson.

Finally she turned on her heel and stalked off to get her lunch. The other Clovers followed her—waddling away like a line of yellow ducklings, Sara thought. She was sure the Stars hadn't heard the last quack from Holly Hudnut.

◄ 3 ►
Holly Hudnut
Declares War!

Even if they wanted to, there was no way
for the Stars to avoid Holly and the other
Clovers for the rest of the day.

In the lunchroom the Stars took their
usual table by the window. The Clovers
were sitting together too, a few tables away.
The cafeteria was so noisy that the Stars
couldn't hear what the Clovers were saying
to each other. But they didn't need a mind
reader to guess that Holly and the others
were talking about them.

"Gee—I feel awful about making our class
lose," Karen said to her friends. She'd gotten the school lunch today. It was always
the same on Monday—sticky ravioli with

peas, a roll and butter, fruit salad, and milk. She didn't feel very hungry and just ate the peas off the ravioli.

"You didn't make us lose, Karen," Amy insisted. "If anyone did, it was Holly."

"Even if she stepped on your feet by accident—which I *doubt*," Jan said, munching on some potato chips, "she could be honest enough to admit it."

"Miss Perfection *admit* she did something wrong?" Sara said. "That'll be the day."

"I'd call her a slimy snake—but it would be an insult to reptiles," Beth said, finally making Karen smile.

"I'd call her a slimy, two-headed, one-eyed Zigblat, but it would be an insult to space aliens," Karen added.

Laughing at their jokes about Holly, the Stars didn't even notice that the Clovers had finished their lunch and were walking toward their table.

"Watch out, stand clear—" Holly called out loud enough for the whole lunchroom to hear as she passed by the Stars' table. "It's the notorious *Falling* Stars. Usually they only fall down on each other, but who knows who'll be their next victim."

Kids at other tables had heard Holly and turned to see what would happen next.

"Oh, gross—here they come," Beth said to her friends. "I think I'm going to gag." She stuck her tongue out and put her hands around her throat as if she were choking.

Amy, Karen, and Jan started laughing at Beth, but Sara just glared at her twin, her cheeks getting pinker by the second.

"Beth—" It was bad enough that the whole lunchroom was staring at them. Sometimes Beth acted so silly she made things even worse.

"Just ignore them and they'll go away," Sara whispered to her friends.

But no such luck. The Clovers weren't ready to leave quite so quickly.

"Hey, Stars—I hear Mr. Carson is putting seat belts at your desks so you don't fall right off your chairs," Roxanne Sachs yelled.

"Yeah—and you're all going to have to wear crash helmets," Mary Rose added, giggling at the idea.

"Very funny," Amy said. "You made Karen fall down, Holly. That's why our class lost. But you'd never admit it in a million years."

"Right," Holly scoffed. "I just knew

something like this was going to happen. I
had a feeling the Sugar Tree Acres Rejects
would find some way to ruin field day for
the whole class."

"Ruin field day! We won two ribbons," Jan
pointed out. "The Clovers only won one."

"Big deal," Holly said. "If you think you're
so great, how about a rematch? A tug-of-
war, just us against you guys."

"Great idea," Brenda chimed in. "Only, I
think the Falling Stars are too wimpy to do
it."

"Oh yeah? We'll show you," Beth said. She
was vaguely aware that all eyes in the
lunchroom were on her, but she didn't care.
She got up out of her chair to face Brenda.
"Want to see a wimp? Go look in the mirror."

Sara bit down on her lip and looked at
the faces of her other friends. Amy and Jan
looked as eager to take up the Clovers'
challenge as Beth. But Karen was quiet and
stared down into her cold ravioli. Maybe it
was wrong of Beth to just blurt out an answer for everyone before they had talked it
over, Sara thought. But it was too late now.

"We'll meet you on Saturday morning,

right here at school," Amy said. "No problem, Holly."

"No problem for us, you mean," Holly said. She glanced over at her friends, and they all nodded in agreement.

"And if the Stars lose, we get to take over your clubhouse for a whole month," Roxanne called out.

The Stars looked at each other. Jan suddenly felt a giant lump in her throat, and she was sure the others felt the same. Meeting the Clovers for a rematch was one thing. But let the Clovers have their clubhouse if they lost? That was going a little too far.

"Uh—we want to talk it over a second," Jan said to Roxanne. "What do you think?" she whispered to the others.

"If we don't say it's okay," Amy whispered back, "it'll look like we think we're going to lose for sure."

Karen wasn't so sure the Stars *would* win. But she didn't want to say that out loud right then.

"Let's make a bet back," she suggested. "They have to give us their clubhouse for a month too if they lose."

"Who wants their dumb old clubhouse?" Beth said. "It's just a stuffy little room over Holly's garage."

"Wait—I've got it!" Amy's eyes lit up and she practically bounced up and down in her seat. "If the Clovers lose, they have to come to school wearing T-shirts that *we* make for them. Ones that say 'The Stars Are the Greatest.' "

"Brilliant!" Jan said, and the others all agreed it was a stroke of genius.

When Amy told the Clovers what their part of the bet had to be, Holly and her friends made the most horrible faces, proof to the Stars that Amy's idea would be perfectly horrendous torture to them.

"Yuck—I'd rather die than wear anything from Amy Danner's closet," Sue Pinson said. She was the mousiest in Holly's group, but she did have nice clothes.

"Don't worry," Holly promised. "How can we end up wearing any of their ugly T-shirts? We'd have to lose, and that couldn't possibly happen."

"Not in a zillion years," Mary Rose agreed.

The terms of their showdown match were set. Everyone in the lunchroom started talking at once. The Clovers stalked off.

They looked as pleased with themselves as if they'd *already* won.

. . .

As usual, the Stars met in their clubhouse after school that afternoon. The cozy stone cottage was truly a special place, and they loved hanging out there. Before they had fixed it up, it had been broken down, overgrown with weeds, and even a little spooky looking. But the Stars had known it could be nice if they worked on it. They earned all the money to fix it themselves by working at odd jobs around the neighborhood, and Jan's uncle, who was a carpenter, helped them repair it.

Nobody had known it at the time, but the clubhouse had been built over seventy years ago by one of River Grove's founders, J. D. Ellison. It had been the playhouse for a little girl named Evelyn Topping. Evelyn Topping was still alive and one of River Grove's most well-respected citizens.

She was an old woman and a bit eccentric at times. But she liked the Stars, and when she found out they had fixed up her old playhouse, she told them that they could use it for as long as they liked.

Jan had made some of her special double-fudge brownies for her family over the weekend. She had saved some for her friends and brought them to the clubhouse on a paper dish covered with tin foil. Jan's brownies were the perfect food for thinking through a big problem—and winning their bet with the Clovers was about the biggest the Stars had faced yet.

"Holly was always jealous of our club-house," Amy said to the others. "No wonder it was the first thing the Clovers thought of as a bet."

"I can't stand the idea of the Clovers being in our clubhouse. Not for a month. Not even for a minute," Beth said, biting into her brownie.

"Don't worry, Beth. It'll never happen," Sara promised her.

"I hope not." Karen wanted to sound as sure of winning as the others did. But she couldn't help feeling a bit nervous. Maybe because she was the one who had started the whole pileup this morning. She knew how easily things could go haywire, just when you thought you'd won. "I mean—I'm sure we'll beat them, too, but . . . they do have Mary Rose. She's pretty strong," Karen added quietly.

"They might have the brawn, but we have the brains," Sara said in a serious tone. She had once heard that line in a movie and had been waiting for a chance to say it out loud ever since. She'd also jotted it down in her notebook to use in her novel, imagining that Sean MacNeill could say it to his pirate friends when he was stuck in his next life-or-death adventure. Of course, just when things looked bleakest, Sean would come up with some brilliant scheme to save his crew. He loved Tiffany too much to ever let himself die without even kissing her once and telling her the truth—he wasn't really a pirate.

"All we have to do is practice. When I went to camp last summer, I was in bad shape," Amy told the others. "But after I worked out for a few weeks, I got really strong."

"Only we don't have three weeks to work out in the woods. We only have tomorrow," Jan pointed out. "It's not nearly enough time to really train."

She knew that her brother started training for football season in July. What could the Stars do to improve their chances of beating the Clovers by Saturday?

"I read this book once called *Visitor from Beyond,* about a space alien who comes down to check out Earth. He looks perfectly normal most of the time. Except for this special trick he has of growing eyes in the back of his head if he's being followed. Or growing extra legs if he's chased, or more arms if he gets in a fight," Karen told the others. "Too bad we can't do that."

"A few extra arms and legs would help win a tug-of-war, I guess," Sara said. "But then all our clothes would look pretty funny," she added with a giggle.

"Yeah, but it would be easier to do things. You could clean up your room or do homework in a flash," Karen said. "Or ride a bike and read at the same time."

"Well, growing extra arms and legs by Saturday is out. But maybe we should do some exercises," Jan said with a shrug. "Anything's better than nothing, I guess."

"My mother watches this show every morning called *Wake-Up Workout with Wanda Monroe.* Why don't we meet before school at my house and do it together?" Amy said. "We're not going to turn into Hulk-ettes overnight, but it might help."

The others thought it was a good idea and agreed to meet at Amy's house the next morning if her mother said it was all right.

"I think we should practice, too," Beth said. "We don't want to make the same mistake and fall down all over each other again."

The very suggestion made the others cringe with embarrassment. That couldn't possibly happen again. Could it?

"There's some rope in our garage left over from when my dad hung our tire swing," Karen said. "I'll ask if we can borrow it for a few days."

"What we really need is a secret strategy," Sara said. "If we want to win, we need a plan."

Sara took out her notebook. On the top of a clean page she wrote: SECRET STRATEGY TO BEAT THE CLOVERS.

The girls were quiet for a moment, munching on their brownies. It was hard to come up with a surefire plan for out-smarting the Clovers.

"How about if we wear cleats on our sneakers, like baseball players?" Jan said.

"Then we could really dig our feet in and they won't be able to budge us."

"That would be perfect. Except it isn't exactly fair," Karen pointed out. "I'm sure the Clovers would get mad and say we were cheating."

"Yeah—guess you're right," Jan agreed. It was a good idea, but it solved the problem as much as Karen's wild story about growing extra arms and legs.

"We don't have to think of a plan right this minute," Sara said. "We have loads of time until Saturday morning. I'm sure we'll come up with something great."

No matter how confident Sara sounded, the others knew that two days wasn't exactly loads of time.

"Don't worry—" Beth picked the last crumb of brownie off the paper dish and popped it into her mouth. "We'll figure out something that'll just blow those Clovers away."

Beth sounded very sure that the Stars would win. She didn't even want to imagine what would happen if they lost.

Nobody did.

◀ 4 ▶

The Stars Get Tough

The next morning Jan, Karen, and the Greenfield twins came to Amy's house before school to "wake up and work out" with the Wanda Monroe show. Amy hadn't told her mother the real reason the girls were suddenly so interested in exercising together, but Ms. Danner didn't mind them coming over.

The girls tried their best to keep up with the routine. But the "early morning fitness queen"—which was how Wanda was introduced by the show's announcer—did a lot of exercises they'd never done before in gym with Mrs. Franks.

"Now here's a great one for firming up your bottom and trimming those late-night snacks off your hips," Wanda said.

"This is dumb." Karen sat up while the others lay on their sides, counting out loud and kicking the air. "We don't even have hips."

Ms. Danner started laughing and had to stop her leg lifts. The other girls agreed with Karen, though, that Wanda's routine wasn't exactly designed to help a person toughen up for a tug-of-war. Instead of watching the rest of the show, they decided to jog around the block. Afterward they each ran back home to change for school.

In the Greenfield house the kitchen was action packed, as usual. Mrs. Greenfield was trying to serve breakfast, sew a button on Amanda's Brownie uniform, and get all seven people in the family off to start the day. Sara and Beth were the oldest. Then there was Amanda, who was in second grade, Jeffrey, who was five, and the new baby, Jessica. Amanda and Jeffrey were eating cereal. Jeffrey was splashing his with his spoon while Amanda dug through the cereal box for the toy surprise. Beth and

Sara breezed through the back door and, as they passed the table, grabbed some toast.

Jessica was in her playpen in the living room. The TV was on, tuned to her favorite show, *Gilda Goose's Neighborhood.* When she saw her big sisters, though, she waved her arms and squealed.

"Hello, baby-munchkin." Beth could never resist her baby sister. She had strawberry-blond curls and big brown eyes. She was so sweet and cuddly, like a puppy, Beth thought. She walked over to the playpen and picked Jessica up.

"What are you doing, funny face?" Sara asked Jessica. "You want to come to school with us today?"

Jessica gurgled happily and reached for Sara's nose.

"Wouldn't that be outrageous?" Sara asked Beth.

"Maybe we can bring her in one day and tell Mr. Carson that she's our science project," Beth said, letting the baby pull her hair.

"Our science project?" Sara knew that she and her sister were identical on the outside, but sometimes the wildest ideas popped out of Beth's mouth. Their brains sure weren't identical.

"Why not? Tommy Tyler is growing a plant out of an avocado pit and Kristy Pratt is watching how tadpoles turn into frogs. We can say our experiment is growing a baby sister."

"Right." Sara shook her head and started toward their bedroom to change. "You'd better put her back or we'll be late for school."

"In a second," Beth said. Gilda Goose was singing her special song, and Beth bounced Jessica up and down while she sang along with the TV. "Ooogla-boogla boo! Yakety, yakety yak! Quackety quack quack quack!"

This week in the Word Power section of their language-arts textbook one of the new vocabulary words had been *audacious*. It meant "adventurous or recklessly bold." That's what Beth is, Sara thought, pulling on her school clothes. Sometimes her sister was *truly* audacious.

The bus ride that morning was much quieter than the one the day before. The Stars asked each other the spelling words that Mr. Carson was going to test them on that morning.

"Catastrophe," Karen asked Amy. It wasn't on the regular list, but it was one of the bonus words.

"C-a-t-a-s-t-r-o-p-h-e," Matthew Ellis blurted out in a rush, leaning over the girls' seat. Matthew always liked to prove how smart he was, and he always eavesdropped on the girls' conversations. "Definition: what will happen if the Stars lose their bet with the Clovers."

"How do you know about that?" Amy asked him.

"Everybody knows." Pete McBride shrugged and put the earphones for his Walkman around his neck. "I bet the whole fifth grade will come Saturday morning to watch." Then, pretending his tape player was a microphone, Pete slipped into his sportscaster imitation. "Ladies and gentlemen, here we are at River Grove Elementary School for the slug-fest of the century!—"

The girls exchanged silent looks. Pete could really get carried away with himself sometimes.

"It's not a boxing match," Jan cut in. "It's a tug-of-war."

"That's even better," Matthew said. "Don't you need some umpires, or referees?"

"Yeah—someone to blow the whistle and make sure nobody cheats?" Pete said to Jan.

"—like us?" Matthew added.

The girls hadn't thought about that. Maybe it wouldn't be such a bad idea. They did need someone to blow a whistle. Jan looked at the other Stars. "What do you guys think?" she asked.

"I think we might need a referee to keep the Clovers in line," Karen said. She knew that Holly could do something outrageous—like stomp on a person's feet—and then totally deny it. Sara and Beth nodded in agreement.

"It's okay with us, if the Clovers say it's okay with them," Amy told the boys.

"Ah-right! It's cool!" Pete and Matthew slipped each other five and bounced up and down on their seat. You'd think someone had just handed them box-seat tickets to the Super Bowl or something, Amy thought.

In school Jan saw Pete talking to Holly right before the bell rang. When everybody had sat down, Pete passed Jan a note. It said, "It's okay with Holly for me and Matt to be referees."

Jan stared down at it a second, then folded it back up and put it in her pocket. She was surprised that Holly had agreed so easily to *anything* the Stars thought was okay. But then she realized that Holly adored any attention from boys—even Pete and Matt. Besides, Holly was so stuck up that she probably thought Pete and Matt both had crushes on her and it would count in the Clovers' favor.

The morning seemed to drag on forever. While Mr. Carson gave the class their spelling test, the sixth grade had begun their field day outside. Mr. Carson kept having to raise his voice over the sixth graders' shouting and cheering. At each cheer, the Stars were sadly reminded of how they had accidentally caused their class to come in second yesterday. And all because of Holly Hudnut.

Right before lunch, while Mr. Carson was going over the reading from their social studies text, Brenda Wallace flipped a note onto Amy's desk. At first she thought

Brenda wanted her to pass it to one of the other Clovers. But when she looked up, Brenda mouthed the words, "Read it."

Amy opened it. It said, "We have some good redecorating ideas for your clubhouse. Can't wait to get started. The Clovers."

Amy was fuming. All she could picture was her giant King Zero poster being torn down and replaced with something corny and Clover-ish, like some dumb-looking horse poster.

She saved the note and passed it around to the other Stars at lunch. It made everyone mad. The situation was getting serious.

But Jan had a surprise for her friends, one she hoped would cheer them up. While they passed around Brenda's note, she waited to tell them about it.

"Oh, let's forget about that dumb note. Listen to this," she said finally. "Last night at supper my brother was telling me how runners 'carbo up' for extra energy the night before a big race—"

"What does 'Garbo up' mean?" Karen frowned, the way she did whenever she was confused. "You mean like the actress Greta Garbo?"

"No, silly," Amy said. "*Carbo,* as in carbohydrates. Foods with starch and sugar, like cookies or spaghetti." Because of her mother, Amy was a regular encyclopedia about nutrition.

"Right, the night before the River Grove Marathon, all the runners get together at the firehouse and eat tons of spaghetti," Beth said.

"Well, you're all invited to my house tonight to 'carbo up' for tomorrow," Jan finally managed to tell her friends. "My mom said I could cook a spaghetti dinner, and that it was okay for everyone to sleep over."

"Hey, that will be great!" Sara said. "We can work on our secret strategy some more," she whispered, glancing over at the Clovers' table.

"We can work on the T-shirts the Clovers are going to wear to school on Monday," Amy added, taking it for granted that the Clovers would lose. "I'll bring the fabric paint and other stuff if you each bring an old shirt to work on."

Beth had a surprise for the other Stars too, something she thought would help beat the Clovers. But she didn't say a word. She just smiled to herself and took a bite of her sandwich. She would wait until tonight to show it to them.

• • •

After school, the Stars changed into their workout clothes again and rode their bikes over to their clubhouse. Karen had brought a length of sturdy rope to practice with, and Jan said her brother might come by to give them some pointers.

The girls decided to warm up first with some jumping jacks and push-ups. Amy had brought her big yellow radio and tape player. She popped in a tape and blasted it. It was King Zero's latest album.

"Hey, hey, goin' to get you—" King Zero warned. "Watch out, baby! Here I come. Got you on the run. You're goin' to see who's number one. Going to get *you*!—"

It was the perfect psych-up tune to raise their spirits, and the Stars sang along with the tape at the top of their lungs, changing King Zero's version to lyrics about themselves and the Clovers.

"Watch out, Clovers. Here we come!" Beth sang in between jumping jacks.

"Goin' to get you! Goin' to get you!" the Stars shouted along with King Zero.

When the song was over, the girls collapsed on the big cushions they had tossed around the clubhouse floor. They were nearly breathless from push-ups, jumping jacks, and laughing so hard. Amy had brought along her camping thermos with ice water, and they passed it around.

"I don't know where my brother is." Jan looked down at her watch. "It's getting late. Let's start without him. Where's the rope you brought, Karen?"

"I left it out here," Karen said as the girls followed Jan outside. "Right near the door . . ." Her voice trailed off as she looked down for the rope.

It was there all right, but not exactly as Karen had left it.

"Look! What a mess—" Karen picked up one end of the coiled rope. It was a huge ball of tangled knots.

"Oh, gross! It feels really slimy, too," Amy said, taking hold of the rope and trying to untangle it. She sniffed her hands. "Smells like . . . hair gel. The kind Roxanne Sachs uses to gunk up her perm."

The Stars knew immediately that the Clovers were the culprits.

"They must have come over here to spy on us," Sara said.

"And we had the tape player up so loud

we didn't even hear them sneak up and mess up our rope," Karen added.

"Maybe we can get the knots out," Beth said. She grabbed the first loose end she could find, but in trying to undo one knot, she accidentally made another. "What a puzzle. This is worse than a Rubik's cube."

"Forget it, Beth. It'll take us a year to unravel it," Jan said.

The Stars were staring glumly at their rope, not knowing what to do, when Richie drove up in the Batemans' pickup truck.

"Hi, girls. Sorry I'm late," Richie greeted them.

"That's all right." Jan sighed. "It doesn't matter. We can't practice anyway. We don't have any rope."

"What happened to this?" Richie poked the tangled rope with the toe of his running shoe. "Good thing I remembered to bring some," he said lightly, making the girls smile again. "I'll go get it. It's in the back of the truck."

Sometimes her older brother could be a real pain, Jan thought. Like when he got on the phone after dinner with his girlfriend and tied up the line for hours. But sometimes—like right now—she was really glad he was around.

For the next hour or so Richie helped the girls with what he called their "technique." He showed them how to get the best grip on the rope and where to put their feet so they wouldn't trip each other up.

They split into sides, with Karen, Beth, and Sara taking one end and Jan, Amy, and Richie on the other. Richie promised he would only pull a little so that it would be a fair match.

They practiced a few times. Richie told them to bend their knees more and lean all the way back. "The trick is to get some leverage," he told them.

The Stars nodded. Jan couldn't help but notice that her friends were listening to her brother as if he were going to give a surprise quiz on the subject any minute. If we ever paid this much attention to Mr. Carson, we'd all have straight *A*'s on our report cards, she thought.

"One, two, three—go!" Richie gave the signal and they pulled, trying to remember what he had said about their hands, knees, and feet. It was a lot to coordinate all at once. They practiced until their arms and legs ached. At first, their practice matches didn't take long. But pretty soon the two teams of Stars were giving each other some real competition.

"Hey—not bad," Richie said finally. "Not bad at all. I was pulling really hard too. You'll do fine tomorrow," he assured them. "You just wait and see."

After Richie left, the Stars went back into their clubhouse.

"We were pretty good that last time," Karen said, bending her arm to check out her muscle.

"We're turning into regular . . . Hulk-ettes," Amy cheerfully declared, checking her own arm muscles.

"The Clovers might take one look at us tomorrow," Sara said, "and chicken out."

"Brawck-brawck! Brawck!" Beth folded her arms like wings and did an impromptu chicken imitation. "This is Holly, doing her sore loser chicken dance after we beat the Clovers tomorrow—"

"Beth—" While the others laughed, Sara gave her sister an exasperated look.

"Well—" Beth shrugged. "I guess we shouldn't count our chickens before they're made into little nuggets and served up at McDonald's."

"I just wish there was some way we could get back at the Clovers for messing up our rope," Amy said.

"As the leader of the robot race on planet Quark once said, winning is the best revenge," Karen said in a thoughtful tone. "And also, make sure you zap out the other guys' microchips," she added.

"The Clovers don't have any microchips in their brains," Amy pointed out. "Probably more like potato chips."

"Or maybe Cheese Doodles." Sara giggled.

"This conversation is making me hungry," Beth said.

"Me too." Jan suddenly checked the time. She hadn't realized it was so late. "Wow, I've got to go home and start cooking. See you guys later."

The girls looked forward to their sleepover at Jan's. They knew they'd improved a lot with Richie's help. But it was still impossible to say for sure how they would do tomorrow against the Clovers.

◄ 5 ►

The Spaghetti Sleepover

When the Stars arrived at the Batemans' house that night, they were greeted by the aroma of Jan's spicy tomato sauce. Richie had gone out with his friends, and Mr. and Mrs. Bateman had eaten their dinner early, so the girls had the kitchen all to themselves.

"This is just like a victory party," Karen said. "Except that we didn't win yet."

"But we will," Beth quickly added. "Especially if we eat even half of that spaghetti," she said, looking over at the huge pot on the stove. "We'll weigh a ton each, like pro wrestlers."

"I guess I misjudged the amount a little,"

Jan said. "I forgot that spaghetti grows when you cook it."

"This stuff is definitely still growing." Amy warily poked a long-handled wooden spoon into the pot. "It looks like something out of a horror movie."

That was all she had to say to get Karen's imagination going. The giant mound of noodles did look kind of ominous.

"I hope it doesn't fight back if we try to eat it," she said. Karen really didn't like spaghetti that much. She would rather have sent out for Chinese food.

"Here goes," Jan said bravely. The spaghetti was a bit slippery and sticky and did fight Jan's attempts to get it onto the plates. But she managed to fill the first plate without too much of it flying around the kitchen.

"I'll set the table," Karen offered.

"I'll help," Beth said. She and Karen quickly found forks, glasses, and paper napkins. Sara and Amy took the plates over to the stove and helped Jan dish out the spaghetti and ladle sauce on top.

"A toast," Amy said once they were all sitting down. She lifted her glass of soda and the others did the same. "To carbo loading—and to the chef, Jan Bateman."

Jan smiled modestly as everyone clinked their glasses together. "And here's to the Stars winning tomorrow," she added.

"And to no Clovers in our clubhouse," Sara said. "Ever."

The girls heartily clinked their glasses together once more after that toast. The very thought of what might happen tomorrow if they lost was almost enough to take their appetites away. But nobody wanted to ruin the party mood, so they all kept their worst fears to themselves.

"Did everyone bring a T-shirt to decorate?" Amy asked the others. "I brought all the fabric markers and other stuff."

"Sara and I didn't have any extra T-shirts," Beth said, glancing with a secret smile at her twin.

"But my mom found two of my father's old undershirts in this bag she has of cleaning rags," Sara finished for her. "They're kind of worn out, and they smell like mothballs—"

"They are truly *gross*," Beth cut in, "which makes them perfect for the Clovers."

The girls were eager to get started on their project. After they finished eating, they quickly cleaned up the kitchen while Jan put the leftover spaghetti away in the biggest bowl she could find.

Up in Jan's bedroom they spread out the art supplies on the floor and got to work. Amy showed them how to put a piece of cardboard inside the T-shirt and pin it so that the lettering with the fabric markers wouldn't get smeared and blurry.

"Okay, all the shirts are going to say THE STARS ARE THE GREATEST on the front," Amy said. "I think we should write it in orange or red so people can see it from far away."

"I'm going to outline mine in sequins," Sara decided. "The Clovers will absolutely hate it," she said cheerfully.

"I'm going to put green and purple polka dots on mine," Karen said. "Like the flag of planet Zigblat."

"Just remember, the *uglier* the better," Jan reminded them.

She put a tape on her cassette player, and the Stars worked away merrily. They wanted to make the T-shirts so horrendously ugly that the Clovers would shrivel from embarrassment when they wore them.

"Hey—I nearly forgot. I have something to show you guys." Beth jumped up and rummaged through her knapsack. "Close your eyes for a second," she told them, and everybody did.

"Beth—?" Sara closed her eyes, then decided to peek between her fingers. What was her sister up to now? Couldn't Beth warn her once in a while when she was going to do something crazy?

"Okay—you can look," she said with a muffled giggle.

They all looked at her at once. At first, she looked like regular old Beth. They couldn't figure out what the big secret was.

Then all of a sudden she lifted her arms and made a funny growling sound. When she opened her mouth, they each let out a shriek and then started laughing. Beth had put on a pair of fake Dracula fangs, the kind the town variety store sold at Halloween.

"Beth, what are you doing?" Sara asked her.

But Beth wouldn't answer. She growled again and came closer. With her curly red hair and freckles she did look pretty wild.

"Back, you beast!" Amy hopped up on

Jan's bed. "All we can give you is some left-over spaghetti—"

Beth growled and clawed the air near Amy's feet, making her jump. Then all of a sudden her fake teeth popped out and fell on the rug. Everybody started giggling again.

"Hey, monster, you lost your teeth," Karen teased.

"They stay in better if you stick a little piece of chewing gum in there first." Beth picked up her teeth and sat down on the floor again. "So? What do you think?" she asked the others eagerly.

Jan looked around the room. Had she missed something? Everyone else looked confused too. "Think about what?" she asked Beth.

"The *teeth*," Beth said excitedly. "Don't you get it? It's our secret strategy!"

"Our secret strategy?" Jan still didn't get it.

"You mean, you think if you wear those fake fangs tomorrow you'll scare the Clovers and make us win?" Amy asked, sounding doubtful.

"Not just me—" Beth was in her knapsack again and pulled out a paper bag. She dumped it out in the middle of the floor. "I got all of us a pair."

For a moment the girls just sat there and stared down at the pile of pink-and-white plastic teeth. Nobody knew what to say. Amy picked up a pair, but she didn't put them in her mouth.

"We are not going to wear those silly teeth, Beth," Sara said. Sara knew she was the one who had suggested they think up a secret strategy. But she hadn't meant fake Dracula fangs.

"Why not?" Beth couldn't understand her objection. "We start the tug-of-war, like normal. Then, right near the end, we show our fangs"—she popped the teeth in again—"g-r-r-r! Surprise attack!"

"I don't know . . . maybe it would work." Jan picked up a pair of the teeth too. "My dad always says surprise plays work the best in football."

"Let's just try them on and see how they look," Amy suggested.

Beth was delighted. Jan and Amy quickly put their teeth on. But Karen and Sara were a bit more hesitant. Finally, with their fake fangs in place, they all lined up in front of the bathroom mirror.

"Okay, on the count of three," Beth said. "One, two, three—"

The girls showed their fangs and growled. Their reflection looked so horrible and funny at the same time that they practially collapsed with laughter on the bathroom floor.

All of a sudden, Mrs. Bateman knocked on the door. "Girls? What's going on in there?"

"My mom," Jan whispered. "Let's try it out on her." The others nodded silently and got ready. "We're fine, Mom—"

Jan opened the door and the Stars growled at Mrs. Bateman. She jumped back with her hand to her throat.

"For goodness' sakes! You scared the living daylights out of me." But she was smiling.

"Sorry," Jan said, pulling out her teeth.

"I'll bet," Mrs. Bateman said with a laugh. "What were you guys doing in there, flossing?"

"Funny, Mom," Jan said, making a face. Her mother *was* pretty funny sometimes—for a grownup.

"Anybody want some brownies and ice cream?"

Of course, everybody did.

"We'll be right down," Jan told her mother.

"Fine." Mrs. Bateman headed back downstairs. "But without those silly teeth, please?" she called back over her shoulder.

"Hey, can you imagine the look on the Clovers' faces if we really wear these things tomorrow?" Amy asked the others with a mischievous chuckle.

"I was just thinking the same exact thing," Jan said, checking out her reflection again from the side. "My mother looked like she was going to jump out of her skin."

"I think it's crazy." Sara shook her head. Then she looked at Beth, the only one who hadn't taken her teeth out yet. "I don't think it will work."

"Why won't it work?" Beth insisted. She had already thought out the fine points of the plan. Right before the tug-of-war started, she explained, they'd go into a huddle and secretly slip in the teeth. Then once things got rolling, Beth would give the signal for the surprise attack.

"It sounds like we might be able to fool them," Karen said thoughtfully. "But don't you guys think it's kind of cheating?"

"Gee—maybe," Jan said.

"Well, it's sort of an unfair advantage, like putting rocks in our pockets or something, isn't it?" Karen explained.

"I don't think so," Amy said with a shrug. "After all, we have to look at their weird Clover faces the whole time—which are scary enough *without* fake teeth, if you ask me."

"True . . . but maybe Karen's right," Beth said, surprising all of them. "If the Clovers say we didn't play fair and get Pete and Matt to say so too," she added, remembering their referees, "we'll lose anyway. I sure don't want that to happen."

Beth suddenly seemed as worried about losing as she had been excited before about her brainstorm. Sara felt sorry for her. Beth's scheme was a little silly, but she was only trying to help.

"Maybe you're right, Beth. Holly and her friends will look for any excuse to say we didn't play fair. Especially if we win," Jan said.

"We'd better not give them such an easy out, I guess," Amy added.

"Don't worry, Beth. We'll win, even without the fangs," Sara told her twin. "And your idea was really neat. Honest."

"Thanks." Beth sighed. She collected everybody's teeth and put them back in the paper bag.

"Don't lose them," Amy said. "You never know when great fake fangs like that might come in handy."

The girls went downstairs for their dessert, then got ready for bed. Jan's room wasn't very big, but there was space enough for all of them to open their sleeping bags and get comfortable.

Jan had a small aquarium on her dresser, and the light in the tank glowed softly in the darkness. The girls talked more about facing the Clovers at the schoolyard the next morning. They were so excited it was hard to fall asleep.

They were sorry that they hadn't come up with a secret strategy tonight that would make them sure to win. But the Stars agreed that even though it would be great fun to try out Beth's scheme, they were going to win this match fair and square.

◄ 6 ►

The Big Showdown— and an Almost Instant Replay

"Wow—look at all those kids!" Karen was the first to see the crowd that had come to watch the showdown between the Stars and the Clovers. The girls rode up to the schoolyard on their bikes Saturday morning at eleven o'clock sharp, but it seemed that they were the last to arrive. "I thought only the Clovers would be here."

Karen had felt nervous enough about the contest with the Clovers. Now, it seemed they were going to have an audience, too.

"It looks like the whole fifth grade is here," Jan said, hopping off her bike. "I think I even see sixth graders."

"This must be Pete and Matt's doing,"

Sara decided. "Pete is such a blabbermouth, he probably sold tickets."

"Well—I don't care who's watching," Beth said. "It'll just mean more cheers for us when we win."

"Beth's right," Karen said. "This is no time for stage fright."

Karen suddenly thought of a book she'd just read about alien beings who actually froze whenever they got scared. They could be right in the middle of something—pulling out a laser gun or calling for help—and before they knew it, *zap*. They turned into gigantic icicles, stuck to the spot. The first warning sign was goose bumps on their skin, she recalled, rubbing the goose bumps on her own arms. As the girls walked down to the crowd of kids near the baseball field, Karen kept telling herself over and over that the Stars were going to win and she wasn't scared at all.

Wearing the same outfits they had on for field day, the Clovers were standing in a cluster, talking among themselves. But once the Stars got there, they turned around and took notice.

"Look, they're finally here," Brenda announced. "We thought the *Falling Stars* were going to chicken out."

"No—they had to stop at their clubhouse this morning," Holly said. "To kiss it goodbye."

Naturally, Holly's joke made the others laugh. But it reminded the Stars how much was at stake and made them doubly determined to win.

"Keep laughing, Clonettes," Amy said. "Wait until you see the T-shirts you're going to wear to school on Monday."

"Right—we look really scared, don't we?" Holly said sarcastically. She crossed her arms over her chest and gave Amy a nasty look.

Amy was unfazed. She had brought the shirts with her in a paper bag and was about to pull one out for the sheer joy of hearing the Clovers squeal with disgust. But Pete and Matthew walked up to the Stars, eager to get the contest started.

"Ready for the big showdown?" Pete asked them.

"Of course we are," Sara said, trying to sound far more sure of herself than she felt.

"Piece of cake," Jan agreed.

Pete and Matthew had taken their jobs as referees seriously and were both wearing whistles around their necks and red baseball caps. Pete was holding an orange plastic flag, Beth noticed, and Matthew was holding a Polaroid camera. She wondered if he was going to take pictures for the sports page in *The River Grove Gazette*.

"What's the camera for?" Beth asked him.

"It could be close. The referees might need to see an instant replay," Matthew said.

"It's a tug-of-war, not a football game," she said.

"It's still sports, and *anything* can happen," Matthew replied. It was clear he thought girls didn't know as much about these things as boys.

"Here's the rope. Let's get started." Jan had brought the rope that had been in the back of her father's pickup truck and handed it over to Pete. Considering what had happened yesterday, the Stars didn't trust any rope the Clovers would bring.

"Looks okay to me." Pete checked the coil of rope, trying to act official. "What do you think, Matt?"

"I think we'd better show it to Holly."

Matthew did sound smart at times. No

matter what the referees said, there would be no tug-of-war if Holly didn't give her okay too.

While the Clovers looked over the rope, the Stars took a moment for a last-minute pep talk.

"Remember what Richie told us—we have to pull together and get . . . um . . . leverage," Jan reminded her friends.

"And bend our knees," Karen added.

"If it feels like we're losing ground, just picture the Clovers in *our* clubhouse," Sara said.

"Why do I suddenly wish I had those fake teeth handy?" Beth sighed.

"Come on, Beth." Amy gave her friend a reassuring pat on the shoulder. "If it makes you feel better, just pretend we're wearing them, okay?"

Beth nodded, but she didn't look like she felt much better. In fact, the Stars were all nervous. Finally Pete and Matthew stretched out the rope, and the girls took their places.

The Clovers looked nervous too. Holly had taken charge as usual and was bossing everyone around. "No, Sue, you stand in back of Brenda. Brenda is behind me. . . ."

While the Stars lined up as they had planned, the Clovers scrambled around, with Holly giving more directions than a traffic light.

"What is this, musical chairs?" Amy said finally. "Maybe we should come back tomorrow, when you have it together."

Acting as if she had all the time in the world, Holly took her place at the front of the Clovers. She was facing Beth, who glared at her.

"Boy, you Stars are pretty eager to lose, aren't you?" Brenda said.

"Just wait and see!" Jan shouted.

"You Clovers are finished. You're history. You're going to be pressed in a book with a lot of other dried-up old weeds!" Amy yelled.

The Clovers started shouting something back, but Pete and Matthew blew their whistles.

"Time out! Time out!" Pete shouted, waving his flag. It didn't really make sense for Pete to be calling a time-out from a put-down session between the two teams, but it worked. At last the Stars and the Clovers were quiet.

"Okay, when I blow my whistle, this tug-of-war is officially started," Pete said. Behind him, Matthew was ready with his camera. "One, two—"

The Stars gripped the rope the special way Richie had showed them. "Bend your knees!" Jan whispered to the others.

"Three!" Pete said, then blew his whistle shrilly. The Stars started pulling with all their might. The kids who had come to watch started cheering, some for the Stars and some for the Clovers.

"Harder, harder!" Beth said, digging in her heels. The Clovers were stronger than she had suspected. But every time she looked at Holly just a few feet down the rope, it made her so mad she felt an amazing new burst of muscle power.

As precious seconds ticked by, the Stars tried to remember all of Richie's tips. They gritted their teeth and leaned back, putting their heart into the battle.

"No Clovers in our clubhouse. No Clovers in our clubhouse . . ." Sara kept repeating to herself under her breath.

The Stars pulled hard. But after a few more seconds, it suddenly felt like the Clovers were pulling harder. The Stars tried their best to hold on. But little by little, the rope began to inch toward Holly and her friends.

The Clovers felt it too. They were just a fraction of an inch away from victory when Holly started shouting directions to everyone.

"Mary Rose, pull harder! Brenda, you're pushing me!" Holly complained to her teammates.

"Holly! You're stepping on my fee—" Before Brenda had even gotten the words out, she fell backward into Sue, who shrieked and fell backward into Mary Rose, who yelled, "Oh, no!" before she fell down under both of them. And of course, they had all let go of the rope.

"Now! Now!" Karen shouted, and the Stars pulled. Pete blew his whistle while Matthew clicked away with his Polaroid camera.

"The official winners—the Stars!" Pete said, waving the orange plastic flag over the Stars.

"Yeah! All right!" The Stars hugged each other, then jumped up and down cheering for themselves. "We did it! We won!"

"The official *losers,* the Clovers," Pete announced, blowing his whistle again.

Holly stared at him, her hands on her

hips. She was fuming, but there was nothing she could say. The Stars had won, fair and square.

"Oh, shut up, McBride. And quit blowing that dumb whistle," she said, putting her hands over her ears.

The other Clovers slowly got up from the ground and brushed themselves off.

"I can't believe it," Mary Rose moaned. "We nearly won."

"We would have. But Holly stepped on my feet," Brenda said.

"I did not!" Holly said to Brenda.

"You did too," Matthew said. "Look." There it was, in color too, a photo finish of the very moment Holly had caused an avalanche of Clovers.

"Give me that," Brenda said, snatching the picture away. "See—I knew it."

"Oh, big deal," Holly said. The other Clovers just glared at her.

"Well, looks like we won," Amy said to Holly. "Time to collect on our bet." She held up her paper bag of T-shirts and rattled it. "Come and get 'em, ladies. T-shirts, made to order."

"Forget it," Brenda said. "We're not going to wear those ugly T-shirts. No way."

"But that was our bet," Jan reminded her.

"So what. You can't *make* us wear them," Holly said.

"Hey, that's not fair," Matthew cut in. For once the Stars appreciated his butting in on their conversation. "A bet is a bet."

"Oh, go away," Brenda told him. "Who invited you here, anyway?"

"Matthew's right. That was our deal," Jan insisted.

"Tough," Holly said. "We're not going to wear your dumb shirts to school on Monday. And that's that."

The other Clovers had seemed mad at Holly a few minutes ago. But now they stood around her with the same old adoring expressions.

Before the Stars could say another word, Holly turned to her friends. "Come on, let's go back to my house. My mom said she'd take us into town for lunch."

The Clovers hopped on their bikes and took off. The Stars knew there was nothing they could do or say to make the Clovers keep their word.

"You guys should have guessed that the Clovers wouldn't keep up their end of the bet," Pete said, and the girls knew he was probably right.

"But we won, and that's what really counts," Jan replied.

"Maybe lightning doesn't strike twice . . . but Holly's feet sure do," Karen said.

"Did you see her face when Matt showed her that picture?" Amy laughed. "That was the best."

"Poetic justice," Sara said.

"More like Polaroid justice," Matthew cut in, admiring the photo of the grand finale again. "I knew this camera would come in handy. Even if some people thought it was a dumb idea," he said, looking at Beth.

"Can we have the photo as a souvenir?" Jan asked him. "It will look great in a special frame, hanging in our clubhouse."

"Sure." Matthew shrugged and handed it over.

"Here—you guys can have the flag too if you want," Pete added. "It's not really a trophy, but sort of like one."

"Gee—thanks!" Beth took the little orange flag and waved it over her head. "Hooray for us! No Clovers in our clubhouse!"

"Let's go back to the clubhouse and celebrate," Sara suggested. The girls thought that was a great idea and rode off on their bikes with a flag-waving Beth in the lead.

The Stars had always loved their clubhouse, but they had never appreciated it more than they did that Saturday afternoon, savoring their victory. Instead of worrying about how the Clovers would redecorate, they hung the flag Pete had given them over the fireplace mantle and picked out the perfect place to hang the photo once it was framed, right next to their giant poster of King Zero.

Now that the worst was over and they had come through with flying colors, the Stars couldn't have been happier. It didn't seem to matter much that the Clovers had backed out of their bargain. By Monday morning, everyone in school who hadn't seen the event firsthand would have heard how the Stars had won. The girls knew they could depend on Pete and Matthew to spread the news.

"We were terrific," Jan said.

"From Falling Stars to Lucky Stars," Sara agreed.

"And from Clovers to Klutzoids," Amy said.

"Winning is the best revenge after all," Beth pointed out.

"And whoever said a picture is worth a thousand words must have been thinking of Holly Hudnut," Karen added, admiring the photo of the Clovers' downfall once more. "Even Holly won't be able to talk her way out of this one."

Laughing together, the Stars had to agree. They could only imagine what Holly would say on Monday. But one thing was for sure. This time they really had gotten the best of the Clovers.